D0525340

Aberdeenshire Library and Information Service
www.aberdeenshire.gov.uk/alis
Renewals Hotline 01224 661511

22 AUG 2016   18 MAY 2017
HQ   HQ

17 MAY 2017
HQ

UMANSKY, Kaye

The big mix-up

Buster Gutt

**Join Buster and his gruesome crew
for more piratical adventures!**

 Be sure to read:
Buster's Big Surprise

... and lots, lots more!

The Big Mix-up

Kaye Umansky
illustrated by Leo Broadley

SCHOLASTIC

Scholastic Children's Books,
Commonwealth House, 1-19 New Oxford Street,
London, WC1A 1NU, UK
a division of Scholastic Ltd
London ~ New York ~ Toronto ~ Sydney ~ Auckland
Mexico City ~ New Delhi ~ Hong Kong

First published by Scholastic Ltd, 2003

Text copyright © Kaye Umansky, 2003
Illustrations copyright © Leo Broadley, 2003

ISBN 0 439 98179 4

Printed and bound by Tien Wah Press Pte. Ltd, Singapore

10 9 8 7 6 5 4 3 2

The rights of Kaye Umansky and Leo Broadley to be identified as the author and illustrator of this work respectively have been asserted by them in accordance with the Copyright, Designs and Patents Act, 1988.

☠ Chapter One ☠

The Bad Joke was in port – in disguise!
A flowery tablecloth fluttered in place of
the Jolly Roger. A board had been nailed
over the ship's name. It was decorated with
hearts and read: **THE NICE SHIP**.

Buster Gutt, the pirate chief, stood on the jetty admiring it.

"But why bother?" sniffed Timothy Tiddlefish, the cabin boy, who always had a cold. "Everyone knows it's us."

"Because that's the way 'tis done," said Buster. "'Tis good manners when we're in port."

"But we're a piratical band of cut-throats. We don't need good manners," said Timothy. "*Atishoo!* Sorry!"

"Well, like I say, 'tis tradition," said Buster.

"Let's go," begged
Threefingers Jake,
the bosun. "I'm starvin'.
Let's find a tavern
an' order up a keg
of ale an' a platter
of octopus scratchin's."

"Aye!" chorused Jimmy Maggot the cook,
One-Eyed Ed the lookout and Crasher
Jackson the helmsman.

"Woof!" barked Bowzer, the ship's dog.
He *loved* octopus scratchings.

"Looking for a tavern, gents?" asked a voice. It belonged to a small, ragged, angelic-looking child with masses of golden curls. He was sitting on a lobster pot, carving a toy boat.

"Aye," growled Buster. "Know a good one, lad?"

"You could try *The Sailor's Rest.* That's where most folks go," said the angelic child, helpfully.

"Has it got dirty sawdust on the floor?" demanded Threefingers Jake.

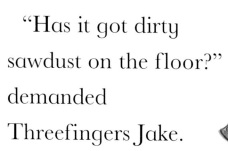

"An' grubby tankards with fingermarks?" chipped in Jimmy Maggot.

"And mucky benches where we can park our sea-weary bums?" asked Crasher Jackson eagerly.

"Oh yes," said the child. "And there's a fight every night and the ale's real cheap." He pointed. "Up that alley on the right. *The Sailor's Rest*. You can't miss it."

"Sounds like our sort o' place," nodded Buster. He tossed the child a penny. "Come on, lads, let's go."

Chapter Two

The *HMS Glorious* was also in port – but
in another, posher part of the harbour,
where there was a better class of wave.
Admiral Ainsley Goldglove, famous
pirate-hunter, came strolling down the
gangplank, waving his gold-gloved hand.

His crew followed behind, in order of importance.

First Officer Crisply Pimpleby marched briskly after the admiral. Then came Monty Marshmallow, the chef, followed by Seaman Scuttle, the deckhand. Private Derek Plankton (nothing special) brought up the rear, dusting as he went.

"Ah, it's good to set foot on land again,"
remarked the admiral, stepping on to
the cobblestones. "What, no cheering
crowds? Funny."

"You said you didn't want cheering
crowds, Admiral," said Crisply Pimpleby,
saluting. "You said you wanted to slip
ashore and spend
a quiet evening
at the nearest
officers' club."

"Quite right, Pimpleby, I did say that.
Yes, I've been too long at sea. What I need
is a hot bath,
followed by a
delicious
meal with
fine wine…"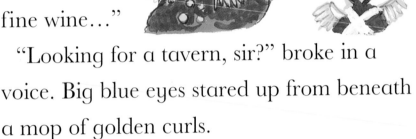

"Looking for a tavern, sir?" broke in a
voice. Big blue eyes stared up from beneath
a mop of golden curls.

"Yes, small boy," said the admiral. "Do
you know of one?"

"*The Sailor's Chest*, sir," said the boy. "'Tis a fine place. Only important gentlemen go there." He pointed to a dark alley. "Up on the left."

"Thank you, lad," smiled the admiral, patting the child's head and handing him a penny.

"Ta," said the angelic child. He smiled sweetly and ran away to hide under an upturned boat and watch the outcome.

"See that mast back there?" said Timothy Tiddlefish, pointing over his shoulder as they started up the alley. "It's got a flag with a gold glove on it."

"Oh aye?" snarled Buster. He spat on the cobbles. "So that jumped-up swankpot Goldglove's in port! Well, let's hope for his sake he don't bump into us."

"Why? What'll
we – *atishoo!* – do?"

"We'll pulverize 'im,
that's what,"
promised
Buster. "We'll
get 'is daft
gold glove off 'im and we'll—"

"Fine," interrupted Threefingers Jake. "But
let's 'ave a drink first. Look. We're here."

They stood outside a grand-looking
building. It had spiked railings and a tall,
imposing door with brass hinges. The sign
above it read:

SAILOR'S REST

MEMBERS ONLY

"Looks a bit posh," remarked One-Eyed Ed. "Think they'll let us in?"

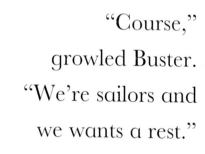

"Course," growled Buster. "We're sailors and we wants a rest."

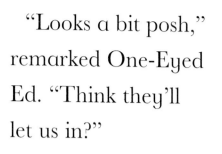

"But we're not members," said Timothy Tiddlefish.

"So? 'Tis two outta three. Oi! You in there! Open up! Kick the door in, Crasher."
Crasher kicked the door in.

Chapter Three

Meanwhile, Admiral Ainsley Goldglove and his crew walked up the dark alley leading to *The Sailor's Chest*. The admiral was talking about Buster. He had wanted to bring him to justice for some time. So far, Buster had avoided capture, and it niggled.

"That Gutt," he muttered, fingering his gold glove. "I'll get him yet. It's only a matter of time. He's slipped the net once too often."

He stopped and stared down the alley. "You know, I was almost sure I saw *The Bad Joke* back there, but it can't be. It had a flowery flag and was called *The Nice Ship*."

"Ridiculous name for a ship," said Crisply
Pimpleby.

"Silly," agreed Monty Marshmallow and
Seaman Scuttle. Private Derek Plankton
said nothing. He thought it sounded – well,
nice.

"Is this right, sir?" asked Crisply
Pimpleby. "It's very dingy round here."

"Of course," snapped the admiral. "*The
Sailor's Chest*. There's the sign, over that
door…"

Just then, the door burst open. Two large, hairy, tattooed figures came flying out, and proceeded to grapple in the gutter. From inside came the sound of loud voices raised in song.

"Good heavens," said Admiral Ainsley Goldglove, startled. "How very unpleasant."

"Thrown out for not being members, I reckon," said Seaman Scuttle.

"Quite right too," said the admiral. "Shocking behaviour. In you go, Pimpleby. Spy out the land."

"Aye aye, sir." Crisply Pimbleby turned smartly on his heel and led the way in.

"What d'you mean, members only?" demanded Buster, thrusting his face at a flustered footman in a wig.

The crew of *The Bad Joke* stood in the red-carpeted lobby of *The Sailor's Rest*, eyeing the oil paintings that lined the walls.

Crystal chandeliers hung from the high ceiling. The door hung off one hinge and there was a big hole kicked in the bottom.

The footman watched in horror as Timothy Tiddlefish wiped his runny nose on a wall hanging. Bowzer made a puddle on the carpet.

"I'm sorry, sir, but it's the rule," twittered the footman, nervously.

"Don't give me *rules*," growled Buster. "Me and the boys want ale an' nosh, see." Meaningfully, he fingered the large cudgel in his belt. "An' you're gonna show us where we goes to get it. Right?"

The footman eyed the cudgel.

"Right," he agreed, opening a door. "Follow me, gentlemen." He led them into a room filled with plush armchairs and small tables.

All conversation stopped as the crew entered. They gawped. The room was awash with tricorn hats, gleaming medals and miles of gold braid. In short, it was stiff with admirals!

"Right," said Buster, into the shocked silence. "Where's the ale?"

"I *say*!" honked a tall, thin admiral, raising his monocle. "What's all this? Who are these oafs?"

"Who're you callin' names, Three-Eyes?" demanded Buster, glaring.

"Why, you, sir! You and your piratical-looking crew!"

"What's wrong with pirates lookin' piratical?" snarled Buster.

A gasp went up. A very old admiral with an ear trumpet pointed a quavering finger. *"Pirates!"* he cried, in a reedy voice. *"In the club!"*

Then he promptly passed out.

"Did we hear correctly, sir?" demanded a fat, red-faced admiral with whiskers. "Did you say you are – *pirates*?"

"So what? None o' your business," yelled Buster. "Anyway, I don't like your hat."

There came an angry rumbling at this, followed by the sound of creaking knee joints. Admirals were setting aside drinks and newspapers and getting to their feet.

"Now you've done it," sighed Timothy
Tiddlefish.

He was right.

Chapter Four

Back at *The Sailor's Chest*, things were also going badly for Admiral Ainsley Goldglove. The rough, tough regulars didn't take kindly to his fancy ways. So far, he had been pushed, jostled and jeered at.

One of his medals had been pinched. He was drenched with spilled ale. Someone was jumping up and down on his gold glove.

"Look!" he protested. "Just *stop* it, will you? Give me my glove, you rotter…"

His crew wasn't faring well either. Crisply Pimpleby's watch had been stolen.

Seaman Scuttle's telescope had gone missing.

Monty Marshmallow was being forcibly held down head first in a vat of octopus scratchings and Private Derek Plankton was being rudely mocked for trying to clean the place up a bit.

Right now, a group of tough customers had the admiral backed into a corner and were demanding a song.

"I can't sing, I tell you!" he protested.

"Ah, go on! Give us a laugh."

"No! I refuse! Get your hands off me, you unwashed louts!"

This was *not* a good thing to say.

Later that night, Buster and his crew limped back down the alley, heading for their ship. They were bruised, battered and utterly exhausted. The admirals had proved a lot tougher than they looked.

"Fancy gettin' thrown out by a bunch of old admirals," Threefingers Jake was saying. "We'll never live it down, Captain."

"It weren't a fair fight," sulked Buster, fingering his black eye. "We was blinded by their medals…"

He stepped out on to the jetty – and stopped.

Limping towards him was none other than Admiral Ainsley Goldglove, and his equally battered crew!

"Atishoo!" sneezed Timothy Tiddlefish, excitedly. "Look! It's Admiral Goldglove! Are we gonna get him, like you said?"

"I know who 'tis," snapped Buster. "Shut up, Tiddlefish. We ain't seen 'im, right?"

"But you said you'd pulverize him! You said … *mwaa!*"

Buster's hairy hand clapped over his mouth.

Hatless, missing one
shoe and soaked
from head to toe,
Admiral Ainsley
Goldglove stood
swaying slightly as
he took in the
unwelcome sight

of Buster and his crew. He wasn't sure he
could make it back to the ship, let alone
have a showdown with Buster.

"Admiral!"
croaked
Crisply
Pimbleby.
"It's him!
Captain
Gu—"

"Pimpleby," said the admiral. He lifted his head and pointed skywards. "Look at that moon. Have you ever seen a more glorious sight?"

"But, sir, you said…"

"*The moon*, Pimpleby. Concentrate on *the moon.*"

And so it was that the two crews slunk silently past each other without a single glance. The admiral's crew dutifully studied the moon.

Buster's crew seemed fascinated by the cobblestones. Silently, they boarded their own ships.

And all was quiet on the jetty. Except for the sound of angelic giggling coming from under a nearby boat.